Lies Don't Fly

written by

Ollie Wheeler III

Lies Don't Fly

Ollie Wheeler @ drwheelerbooks@gmail.com

ISBN 978-1-7333000-0-1

Published by I Am Ollie LLC

Dedication

This book is dedicated to Brian Wheeler Jr., Blake Wheeler, Carmain Desir, Javorie Wilson Jr., and Noah Kemp. It is also dedicated to every child who struggles to fit in. Always know you are accepted and uniquely gifted, talented, and beautiful.

Ollie was going to camp for his first time. Mama packed all the things he needed for Camp Tippy Chunga: his toothbrush, sunblock, flashlight, bug repellant, and undies.

"Spidey tighty-whities? No way, nine-year-olds do not wear those," said Ollie.

"My nine-year-old does," Mama said.

"Aw Ma," grumbled Ollie. "Don't forget to pack Mr. Cuddles."

"Yeah, don't forget me," Mr. Cuddles said.

Tooth Care
Mouth Wash

Mama chuckled and packed Mr. Cuddles, a stuffed, floppy-ear elephant that Ollie had had since he was three. Mr. Cuddles went everywhere with Ollie. He was Ollie's best friend.

"Ollie, the camp bus is here," yelled Papa.

Ollie hugged Mama and Papa, then boarded the bus.

"Hi Ollie," everyone shouted.

Ollie sat next to his friend, Sam, and unpacked Mr. Cuddles.

"Why do you have a silly stuffed animal?" Sam asked.

"My Mom made me bring him," replied Ollie. "I told her silly stuffed animals are for babies."

"Let me hold him," ordered Sam.

"Don't do it. Don't do it," demanded Mr. Cuddles.

Ollie slowly handed Mr. Cuddles to Sam.

"Let's play catch, guys," yelled Sam.

Sam threw Mr. Cuddles to Jeremy. Jeremy threw him to Michael. Michael tossed him to Brian. From one hand to the next, Mr. Cuddles tumbled through the air.

Ollie was sad but did not say a word.

After the boys got tired of throwing Mr. Cuddles around the bus, he was abandoned face down on the floor.

"Campers, welcome to Camp Tippy Chunga," announced Mr. Slouchman, the camp counselor.

When the boys scurried off the bus, Ollie stayed back to get Mr. Cuddles.

"I can't believe you allowed your friends to throw me around like a Frisbee," said Mr. Cuddles. "Some friend you are."

"He just grabbed you! I couldn't help it," Ollie said, and packed him away and ran off the bus.

"Ollie, we're going for a swim," announced Jeremy. "You know how to swim, right?"

"No, no, no! He can't swim," yelled Mr. Cuddles from inside Ollie's backpack.

"Hush, Mr. Cuddles. No one can hear you," whispered Ollie.

"Of course," Ollie said to Jeremy. "Doesn't everyone know how to swim?"

One by one the boys jumped into the lake. SPLISH! SPLASH! SPLISH! SPLASH!

With sweaty palms and his heart racing, Ollie plopped into the lake, landing awkwardly. He began to sink to the bottom.

With his eyes closed, hands waving and legs dangling in the air, Ollie was terrified, so frightened that he did not notice he was safe in Mr. Slouchman's grip.

"Ollie, calm down," said Mr. Slouchman. "The first rule for non-swimmers is always wear a life jacket."

The sun began to set.

"Time to build your tents," announced Mr. Slouchman. "Anyone need help?"

"No," replied Ollie. "Easy peasy lemon squeezy."

"Remember what roams at night when the lights go out: the creepy-crawlies, the bats that fly by night, and the big beasts of the forest," said Mr. Slouchman.

"I'm not afraid of alligators, antelopes, anteaters, or ants," said Sam.

"I'm not bothered by bats, bears, beavers, or beetles," said Brian.

"I'm not concerned about cougars, coyotes, centipedes, or cockroaches," said Jeremy.

"Cockroaches, yuck." The campers chuckled.

"I'm not scared of anything." Ollie said, and shivered.

Ollie and the other campers began to build their tents. Within minutes, beautiful tents were standing strong and tall, but Ollie's tent slumped weak and wobbly.

"Time for bed, guys," announced Mr. Slouchman. "We have a long day ahead of us. Tomorrow, we will hike, fish, collect bugs, and set up a campfire."

"I am the best hiker-fisher-bug collector and campfire setter-upper," said Ollie.

"Great, Ollie, you can lead the group tomorrow," said Mr. Slouchman.

"Yay, Ollie," the campers cheered.

"Oh no," Ollie thought. "I don't know anything about hiking or fishing, and I hate bugs."

Ollie got into his tent and unpacked Mr. Cuddles.

"It took you long enough," said Mr. Cuddles. "I get cramped in backpacks."

"Oh Mr. Cuddles, I'm in big trouble," said Ollie. "I told everyone that I can hike, fish, and catch mushy-gushy gooey bugs."

"Bugs, yummy, yummy in my tummy," said Mr. Cuddles.

"This isn't a joking matter," whined Ollie. "I tell you Mr. Cuddles, I am in big, big trouble."

"Ollie, you don't have to be ashamed of who you are. Just be you," explained Mr. Cuddles.

"I don't think that's a good idea," grumbled Ollie. "No one will think I'm cool."

"It's a perfect idea, you'll see," said Mr. Cuddles, and the tent came tumbling down.

Everyone was awakened by the tent collapsing. Mr. Slouchman and the campers ran over to Ollie's tent.

"Are you okay?" Mr. Slouchman asked, as Ollie arose from under the tent with Mr. Cuddles in his arms.

"What happened to your tent?" Michael asked.

"First the London Bridge, now Ollie's tent." Jeremy laughed.

"Why are you holding that silly stuffed animal again?" Sam asked.

"His name is Mr. Cuddles and he's my friend," said Ollie. "I'm sorry for not telling the truth earlier. I wanted you all to think I was cool. As a matter of fact, I can't swim. I've never put up a tent. I've never been hiking, fishing, or near a campfire, and I hate bugs."

"Ollie, you never have to lie to be cool," said Sam. "We like you whether or not you can swim, hike or put up a tent. Even if you still play with silly stuffed animals, we still think you're pretty cool."

The other campers agreed with Sam and huddled around Ollie.

"Now, help him put up his tent before the creepy-crawlies and the beast of the forest have you all for dinner," said Mr. Slouchman.

In no time Ollie's tent was up and the campers returned to their tents.

"Mr. Cuddles, you were right. My friends like me just the way I am," said Ollie.

"Lies don't fly, but elephants with floppy ears do," said Mr. Cuddles. "I think you have learned your lesson. It is time that we say goodbye."

"Please don't leave me," Ollie said. "I need you."

"You don't need to lean on me anymore," Mr. Cuddles said. "Just remember to always be true to yourself."

Mr. Cuddles crouched low, and then soared up. Up, up and far away into the sky, Mr. Cuddles rocketed away. Ollie was stunned. He had never seen Mr. Cuddles fly. With tears in his eyes, Ollie waved his final goodbye to Mr. Cuddles.

Then Ollie went to sleep, dreaming of learning how to hike, fish, and even how to catch icky bugs.

Made in the USA
Columbia, SC
24 August 2020

17574936R00022